TRAINS DON'T SLEEP

Freight Train

Passenger Train

Circus Train

For Yoni, this book began with you.

And for Sam, who likes to go, Go, GO! —A.W.R.

✿ ✿ ✿

For Liam—I'll always go looking for trains with you. —D.G.

Text copyright © 2017 by Andria Warmflash Rosenbaum

Illustrations copyright © 2017 by Deirdre Gill

www.hmhco.com

The text of this book is set in Arquitecta.

The illustrations are oil on paper.

Library of Congress Cataloging-in-Publication Data is on file.
ISBN 978-0-544-38074-5

Manufactured in China
SCP 10 9 8 7 6 5 4 3 2 1
4500640597

TRAINS DON'T SLEEP

Written by Andria Warmflash Rosenbaum

Illustrated by Deirdre Gill

HOUGHTON MIFFLIN HARCOURT
Boston   New York

Trains are humming, coming near,
Coupled cars from front to rear.
Rumbling, grumbling, screech and squeal,
Rolling, trolling wheels on steel.

Puffing, chuffing, never yawning,
Climbing hills as day is dawning.

Trains don't sleep—
They **CLANG** and **HOOT**,
Reaching stations on their route.

Quiet town to noisy city,
Looming large and strong and gritty.

Passengers, please find a seat,
Ride the rails, and rest your feet.

Trains don't sleep—they need to tow,
Freight and flat cars in a row.

Tender, reefer, logging car,
Built to last and travel far.

Hopper, boxcar, auto rack,
Bridges, tunnels, forest track.

Sky-high trestle,
Canyon sights.
Trains are not afraid of heights.

Through the wind—in rain or snow,
Trains will trudge and *go, Go, GO!*

Transport tractors, trucks, and cranes.
Zoom past traffic stuck in lanes.
Trains don't sleep—they need to lead.
Roaring, rushing, gaining speed.

Flashing lights. Crossing gate.
Sorry, cars, you'll have to wait!

Circus tour with tents and crew,
Elephants and tigers, too.

Poodles, ponies, bears that dance,
Clever clowns in checkered pants.

Down a mountain,
Bold and brave,
Sweep by sheep and share a wave.

Shining headlights journey home,
Rocking slightly as they roam.
Trekking toward the setting sun,
Trains are always on the run.

Give the brakes a gentle push.
Wheels will whisper,
SHUSH, *SHUSH*, SHUSH.
Calm the engine, idle cars,
In the yard beneath the stars.

Good night, travelers,
Off to bed.
Dreams await you just ahead.

Moving on, trains huff and heave,
Knowing that it's time to leave.
Trains don't sleep—they roll away,
Racing toward a brand-new day.

GLOSSARY

Autorack: railcar with racks used to carry cars.

Boxcar: an enclosed railcar with sliding doors, made to hold large crates and bulky boxes.

Caboose: the last railcar, usually painted red.

Circus Train: a train that transports circus performers, equipment, and animals.

Engine: the railcar that powers a train. Engines can be powered by steam or a combination of diesel gas and electricity.

Flat Car: a flat trailer that carries lumber, steel, and large metal containers.

Freight Train: a train that transports heavy things such as cranes, crates, and machinery.

Hopper: a specially shaped railcar used to carry coal, gravel, or grain.

Passenger Train: a train that carries people from place to place.

Reefer: a refrigerated boxcar that keeps food cold.

Steam Train: a train that runs on steam made by burning coal or oil.

Stock Car: a railcar that carries live animals.

Tender: a railcar attached to the engine, made to cary fuel and water.

Trestle: a bridge for trains.

Yard: a large area of tracks where trains are loaded, unloaded, and stored.